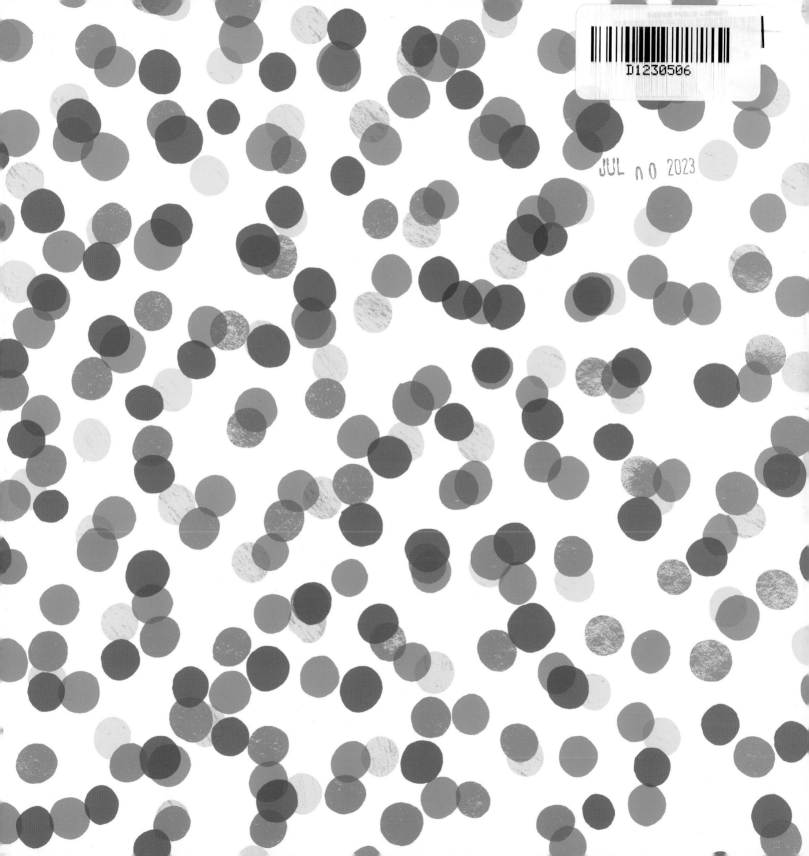

To Christine
–C.B.

For Anouk and Anna.
May your childhood roll
like this little pea.
–M.A.

Roll, Roll, Little Pea
This edition published in 2023
by Red Comet Press, LLC, Brooklyn, NY

First published as *Rouli Rouli Roulette*
Original French text by Cécile Bergame
Illustrations by Magali Attiogbé
© DIDIER JEUNESSE, Paris, 2021
English translation © 2023 Red Comet Press, LLC
Translated by Angus Yuen-Killick

This work received support for excellence in publication
and translation from Albertine Translation,
a program created by Villa Albertine
and funded by FACE Foundation.

Library of Congress
Control Number:
2022937268
ISBN (HB): 978-1-63655-044-2
ISBN (EBOOK): 978-1-63655-045-9

22 23 24 25 21 26 TLF 10 9 8 7 6 5 4 3 2 1

Manufactured in China

RED
COMET
PRESS   RedCometPress.com

ROLL, ROLL, ROLL

LITTLE PEA

CÉCILE BERGAME
MAGALI ATTIOGBÉ

TRANSLATED BY
ANGUS YUEN-KILLICK

RED COMET PRESS ● BROOKLYN

In the kitchen
a little girl shells peas.

The peas roll between
her fingers and, *plop*,
they fall into the bowl.

Look, a little pea has escaped!
The girl does not see it.
IT ROLLS AWAY!

ROLL, ROLL, LITTLE PEA,
across the tiles and under
the sideboard.

Under the sideboard,
there is a mouse.

The mouse would
like to **TASTE** the pea . . .

**ROLL, ROLL,
LITTLE PEA,**
along the floor and
under the stairs.

Under the stairs there is a cat.

The cat would like to **CRUNCH** the pea . . .

ROLL, ROLL, LITTLE PEA,
over the gravel and
into the garden.

In the garden
there is a rabbit.

The rabbit would
like to **NIBBLE**
the pea . . .

ROLL, ROLL, LITTLE PEA,
down the path and into some straw.

In the straw
there is a hen.

The hen would
like to **PECK** the pea . . .

ROLL, ROLL, LITTLE PEA,
over the ground
and into the mud.

In the mud
there is a pig.

The pig would
like to **MUNCH**
the pea . . .

ROLL, ROLL, LITTLE PEA,
across the grass
and into the forest.

In the forest
there is a wolf.

The wolf
would like
to **DEVOUR**
the pea . . .

ROLL, ROLL, LITTLE PEA . . .

along the trail and . . .

plop! It drops into a hole.

TIME passes.

RAIN falls.

The **SUN** shines.

And then one morning,
the little girl finds the
little pea again.
VOILÀ!

MAGALI ATTIOGBÉ
was born in Togo, West Africa, and
moved to France as a young child.
She has worked as an illustrator,
mostly of children's books, for many
French publishers.

CÉCILE BERGAME
is a children's book writer
from Lyon, France, who
focuses on the oral tradition
of storytelling for
young children.